Little MONSTERS

LITTLE MONSTERS, VOLUME 1. October 2022. Published by Image Comics, Inc. Office of publication: PO BOX 14457, Portland, OR 97293. ISBN: 978-1-5343-2318-6

Publication design by Steve Wands

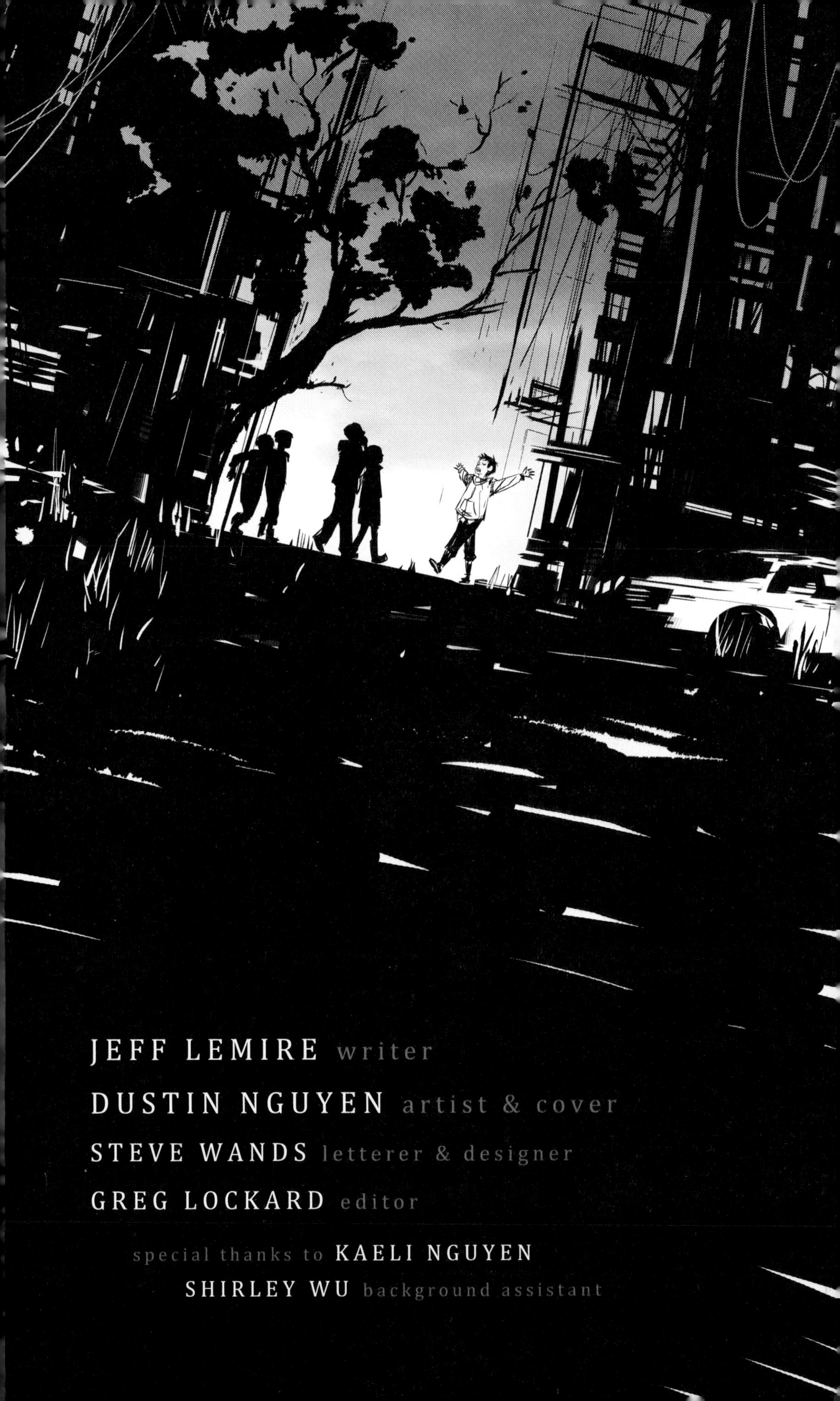

JEFF LEMIRE writer

DUSTIN NGUYEN artist & cover

STEVE WANDS letterer & designer

GREG LOCKARD editor

special thanks to KAELI NGUYEN

SHIRLEY WU background assistant

THESE ARE THE CHILDREN.

ROMIE.

YUI.

LUCAS.
HEY.
HEY.
WHATCHA DOING?
NOTHING. JUST WORKING ON A SONG.
OH.

COOL.
MIND IF I JUST SIT HERE AND LISTEN?
WHATEVER.

YOU WANNA GO PLAY CAPTURE THE FLAG OR SOMETHING? I THINK BILLY AND VICKIE ARE GONNA PLAY.
NAH.
COOL.

YOU FIRST.
NO WAY! THIS WAS YOUR IDEA.
WAS NOT!

IT WAS, TOO! AND NOW YOU'RE CHICKENING OUT! YOU ALWAYS DO THIS!
I'M NOT CHICKENING OUT.

OKAY, WE GO *TOGETHER* THEN. COUNT OF THREE. DEAL?

...
FINE.

ONE... TWO...

THREE!

--UNGH!

HA HA HA! YOU ARE SUCH A LOSER!

I SAID ON THREE!

NO WAY! IT'S ALWAYS ONE, TWO, THREE, AND THEN WE JUMP WHEN YOU SAY GO!

RONNIE & RAYMOND.
GET DOWN HERE AND HELP ME. GONNA TAKE ALL DAY TO HEAL.

BILLY.

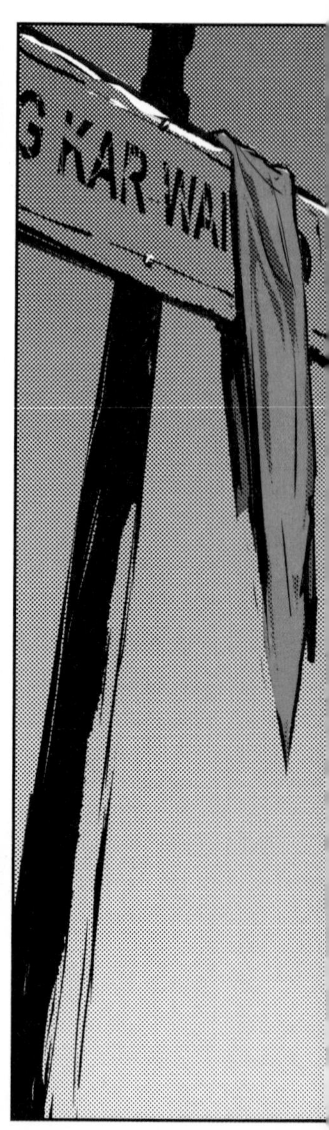

HEY! HE'S GOING FOR IT! *HE'S GOING FOR IT!*
BATS.

I GOT HIM!
VICKIE.

RUN!

--UNGH!

I GOT IT!
NO WAY! I TAGGED YOU FIRST.

I SAW IT, BILLY! SHE TAGGED YOU FIRST!

SHUT UP, BATS.

YOU SHUT UP! SHE GOT YOU. YOU'RE OUT. **WE WIN.**

WHATEVER.

WHAT? YOU'RE ***QUITTING?*** DON'T YOU WANT TO PLAY AGAIN?
NOT REALLY.

WHAT'S YOUR PROBLEM?
NOTHING. IT'S JUST... GETTING ***BORING.***

LUCAS, DO YOU EVER KEEP TRACK OF ALL THE SONGS YOU WRITE?

NAH. NOT REALLY. I PLAY THEM FOR A WHILE AND THEN I KIND OF FORGET THEM AND WRITE NEW ONES.

YOU THINK YOU'VE EVER WRITTEN THE SAME SONG TWICE?

...

HUH. I DON'T KNOW. MAYBE?

I USED TO KEEP TRACK OF HOW MANY BOOKS I HAD. BUT NOT ANYMORE.
IT'S WEIRD WHAT STUFF WE REMEMBER AND WHAT THINGS WE DON'T, HUH?

I STOPPED WORRYING ABOUT THAT A LONG TIME AGO, YUI. JUST SORT OF LET IT GO AND BE IN THE MOMENT.

...OTHERWISE IT ALL JUST GETS *TOO BIG.*

GOT TWO.

ONE.

WHAT HAPPENED TO YOU?
FELL OFF THE ROOF.

HE DIDN'T FALL, HE JUMPED LIKE AN IDIOT.

YOU ARE SUCH A LOSER!
--HEY!

ARRRGH! MY LEG!
SHUT UP! DOESN'T EVEN HURT!

ONE OF THESE NIGHTS YOU TWO ARE GOING TO KILL YOURSELVES.

GOD! AREN'T YOU GUYS SICK OF THIS?
SICK OF WHAT?
THIS! DOING THE SAME STUFF EVERY NIGHT.
CAPTURE THE FLAG, TAG. JUMPING OFF BUILDINGS. ALL OF IT.
GAWD. DON'T START ON THIS AGAIN, BILLY.
WHAT?! THERE'S A WHOLE WORLD OUT THERE. I JUST WANNA GO SOME-WHERE ELSE! DO SOMETHING ELSE.

THERE IS NOTHING OUT THERE. BESIDES, WE GOTTA STAY HERE SO *HE* CAN FIND US WHEN HE COMES BACK.

YOU *REALLY* STILL THINK HE'S COMING BACK? GROW UP, BATS.

OF COURSE HE'S COMING BACK!

IT'S BEEN, WHAT, A HUNDRED YEARS NOW? MAYBE MORE?
SO?

SO, IF THE ELDER'S STILL OUT THERE, WE'D HAVE HEARD FROM HIM BY NOW. FACE IT, GUYS, WE ARE *ON OUR OWN.*

KRKT

WHAT DO YOU GUYS WANNA PLAY TOMORROW? WANNA GO TO THE STADIUM AGAIN AND PLAY WAR?
NAH. TAKES TOO LONG TO WALK DOWN THERE.
theater
TIN STARS

YOU TWO ARE ***SO LAZY.***

WHAT ARE YOU GUYS TALKING ABOUT?
SAME STUFF WE ***ALWAYS*** TALK ABOUT.

GETTING EARLY. WE BETTER GET INSIDE.

HEY, WHERE'S ROMIE?

TSK. THEY'RE PROBABLY DOING THEIR STUPID DRAWINGS AND LOST TRACK OF THE TIME AGAIN.

WELL, THEY BETTER GET BACK SOON. IT'S ALMOST MORNING.

I'LL GO GET THEM.
YOU SURE? I CAN GO.
NAH. I'M THE FASTEST.

DON'T WORRY. YOU GUYS JUST GO TO BED. I'LL GET THEM.

THESE ARE THE CHILDREN. AND FOR LONGER THAN THEY COULD REMEMBER, THEY'D BEEN ALL ALONE.

YUI.

ROMIE! HEY! IT'S TIME FOR BED!

RONNIE & RAYMOND.

ROMIE?

LUCAS.
KRKT
VICKIE.
ROMIE! COME ON. WE GOTTA GO!

BATS.

THESE ARE THE CHILDREN. THIS IS **THEIR WORLD.**

BUT IT TURNS OUT THEY AREN'T ALONE AFTER ALL.
PLEASE-- PLEASE HELP ME!
AND THIS IS THE NIGHT EVERYTHING WOULD CHANGE.

Black forest.
1763.
WHERE ARE YOU GOING?
GETTING COLD. YES. BUT I'LL BE FEELING BETTER TOMORROW. I--I CAN GET MORE WOOD THEN. THAT AXE IS ALMOST AS BIG AS YOU ARE, MY SWEET. COME.

COUGH COUGH
IT'S NOTHING. I'LL BE FINE. JUST NEED--JUST NEED SOME REST.
STAY WITH ME.
--STAY.

IT COMES AT NIGHT.
CHANGE.

AND CHANGE CAN START WITH **JUST ONE.**
CHILD--

I AM SORRY. I HAVE BEEN TRAVELLING FOR **A VERY LONG TIME** AND I--I WAS SO HUNGRY. THOUGHT HE WAS ALONE.

BUT NOW **YOU** ARE ALONE. YES?

WELL, YOU NEED NOT BE.

YOU NEED NEVER BE ALONE **EVER AGAIN.**

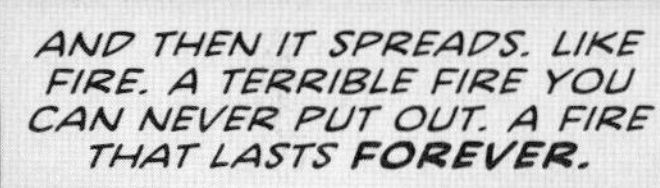
AND THEN IT SPREADS. LIKE FIRE. A TERRIBLE FIRE YOU CAN NEVER PUT OUT. A FIRE THAT LASTS **FOREVER.**

ROMIE.

KRKT

OH!

HEY--IT'S OKAY. DON'T BE SCARED.

I'M NOT GOING TO HURT YOU. ARE YOU--ARE ALL ALONE OUT HERE?

ARE YOUR MOM AND DAD STILL HERE?
I'M JUST LOOKING FOR FOOD...

...BUT THERE IS A WHOLE CAMP OF US. ONLY ABOUT AN HOUR OR TWO AWAY. IF YOU'RE ALONE, MAYBE I CAN HELP YOU--

KRKT
?

ARRRGH!

--HELP! HELP ME!

NO! PLEASE!

AUTO

BILLY.
ROMIE?

PLEASE--CAN YOU HELP ME? FIND SOME PIPE OR REBAR AND HELP PRY THIS OFF?

I--

ARE THERE MORE?

MORE? YES--THERE ARE A FEW OF US. NOT TOO FAR FROM HERE. LOOK, I CAN HELP YOU IF YOU GET ME OUT OF HERE. I CAN BRING YOU TO OUR CAMP, OKAY?

I'M SORRY...

WHAT--
WHAT ARE YOU
DOING?!

WAIT!
NO!

IT COMES
AT NIGHT.
ARRRRGH!

CHANGE.

AND THIS IS THE NIGHT IT ALL CHANGED.

NEVER KNEW WHAT IT WAS *REALLY* LIKE--

HA HA HA!
AND ONE WAS ALL IT WOULD TAKE.

HEY, HAVE YOU SEEN BILLY OR ROMIE YET?
NO. WE WERE COMING TO ASK YOU THE SAME THING.

YOU MEAN THEY *DIDN'T COME BACK?!*

YOU NEVER SHOULD HAVE SENT BILLY OUT THERE, YUI!
ME?! HE VOLUNTEERED!

I WAS JUST WALKING THE BRIDGE. DIDN'T SEE THEM ANYWHERE, AND THE TWINS SAID THEY WEREN'T DOWN BY THE MALL.

THEY'RE FINE. THEY'RE ALWAYS FINE. BILLY'S PROBABLY JUST SLEEPING IN AGAIN, AND ROMIE IS PROBABLY OFF DOING WEIRD ROMIE STUFF.
COME ON. ANYONE WANNA PLAY HIDE AND SEEK OR ZOMBIE TAG?

HOW CAN YOU THINK ABOUT PLAYING STUPID GAMES!?

IT'S OKAY, YUI. BATS IS RIGHT. ROMIE'S SURVIVED LONGER THAN ANY OF US. I'M SURE THEY'RE OKAY.

YEAH, CHILL, YUI. YOU GET SO WORKED UP AS SOON AS ANY-THING CHANGES. RELAX.

BUT IT HAS CHANGED.

THEY NEVER TOLD US.

BILLY, WHERE'S ROMIE?! DID YOU FIND THEM?

BILLY?!

NO. I DIDN'T FIND THEM. BUT I FOUND SOMETHING ELSE, YUI.

WHAT IS GOING ON WITH YOU?
YEAH, MAN. YOU SEEM... DIFFERENT.

UH UH. I FEEL LIKE MYSELF FOR THE FIRST TIME EVER.
THEY NEVER TOLD US WHAT IT WAS REALLY LIKE. THEY KEPT IT FROM US.

I FOUND ONE, YOU GUYS. A PERSON. A MAN. I--I TASTED HIM.

YOU'RE LYING!

NO. I'M NOT. AND I LEFT HIM ALIVE. I LEFT SOME FOR YOU GUYS.

SERVICE
THE CHILDREN COULDN'T AGREE ON MUCH, BUT THEY WERE RIGHT ABOUT ONE THING...

ROMIE HAD SURVIVED LONGER THAN ANY OF THE REST OF THEM.

BUT NOTHING LASTS FOREVER. **NOTHING.**

AND THIS WOULD BE THE NIGHT IT ALL CHANGED. THIS WOULD BE THE NIGHT THAT THEIR **LONG WALK** BEGAN TO END.

AND THAT CHANGE WOULD START WITH **ONE** PERSON.

BUT THAT ONE **WASN'T** BILLY.

AND IT WASN'T EVEN **MY FATHER.**

THE ONE WHO WOULD MAKE FOREVER **END...**

IT WAS ME.
WHO-- WHO ARE YOU?
THWACK

Orange County.
WANDS
LIQUOR
NAIL SPA
COIN LAUNDRY
029.
The Second Pandemic.
HEY KID... HOW'D YOU FIND THAT?! LOOKED ALL OVER THE PLACE.
CAN'T YOU SHARE SOME?!
STAY THE FUCK AWAY.

MOM?
MOM, I FOUND SOME FOOD! BEANS AND CHIPS.
SOME ASSHOLE TRIED TO TAKE THEM, BUT I WAS TOO FAST.
WAKE UP, MOM. SOME FOOD WILL BE GOOD. YOU'LL FEEL BETTER IF YOU EAT.
MOM?

ARRRRGH!
FUCKER! MOTHER FUCKER!

ARE YOU ALONE NOW?

WHAT ARE YOU DOING IN MY HOUSE?! WHAT DO YOU WANT?
DON'T BE SCARED... WE WON'T HURT YOU.

NO ONE WILL EVER HURT YOU AGAIN. IN FACT, I CAN MAKE IT SO YOU NEVER HAVE TO ***KNOW DEATH*** AGAIN.

WHO--
WHO ARE YOU?
WE WERE ALONE, JUST LIKE YOU.
BUT YOU NEVER HAVE TO BE ALONE AGAIN.

BILLY.
THEY NEVER TOLD US! THEY NEVER TOLD US WHAT IT WAS *REALLY* LIKE!

I *FOUND ONE,* YOU GUYS. A PERSON. *A MAN.* I--I *TASTED HIM.*
YOU'RE LYING!
NO. I'M NOT. AND I LEFT HIM *ALIVE.* I *LEFT SOME* FOR YOU GUYS.

ARE YOU--ARE YOU SERIOUS? *DON'T LIE,* BILLY.
HE *IS* LYING.
YEAH. THERE *ARE* NO PEOPLE LEFT!

I'M *NOT LYING!* I LEFT HIM ALIVE AND THERE'S ENOUGH FOR ALL OF US.
YOU GUYS... YOU GUYS HAVE NO IDEA *WHAT IT'S LIKE.*
I CAN'T EVEN EXPLAIN IT!

YOU--YOU'VE CHANGED.
DON'T YOU SEE?! THIS ISN'T WHAT WE'RE SUPPOSED TO BE!

WAIT-- *WHERE'S ROMIE?!*

WHAT? I--I DON'T KNOW.

YOU DON'T KNOW?! YOU WERE **SUPPOSED** TO BE LOOKING FOR THEM!

ROMIE'S FINE! THEY ARE ALWAYS FINE! CAN'T YOU SEE WHAT I'M TELLING YOU HERE? I FOUND FOOD! **REAL FOOD!**

I WANT TO SEE IT... HIM. I WANT TO SEE HIM. SHOW US!

WE NEED TO FIND ROMIE! IF THERE REALLY IS A MAN THEN THERE COULD BE MORE!
I HOPE SO!
YOU **HOPE** SO?! THEY COULD HURT ROMIE! THEY COULD HURT **ALL OF US!**

DON'T YOU GET IT, YUI? THEY CAN'T HURT US... *WE* HURT *THEM.*

SHOW US!

HE'S ONLY TWENTY MINUTES AWAY, PAST THE PARKING LOTS.

WHERE ARE *YOU* GOING?!
WHERE DO YOU THINK? LET'S GO. DON'T YOU CHICKEN OUT ON ME AGAIN.

I--I DON'T KNOW. I DON'T THINK WE SHOULD, RAY. LET'S STAY.
I'M GOING TO LOOK FOR ROMIE. WE *ALL* SHOULD BE.

SUIT YOURSELF, BUT *I'M* GOING WITH OR WITHOUT YOU.
RAYMOND!

IT'S OKAY, RONNIE. THEY'LL BE BACK, BILLY IS LYING. IT'S JUST ANOTHER STUPID GAME OF HIS.

RONNIE?
I'M SORRY, GUYS. I--I HAVE TO BE SURE.

HE *IS* LYING... RIGHT, LUCAS?

LUCAS?
LET'S GO.

"...WE HAVE TO FIND ROMIE."

OH MY GOD! I--I DIDN'T MEAN TO. I--

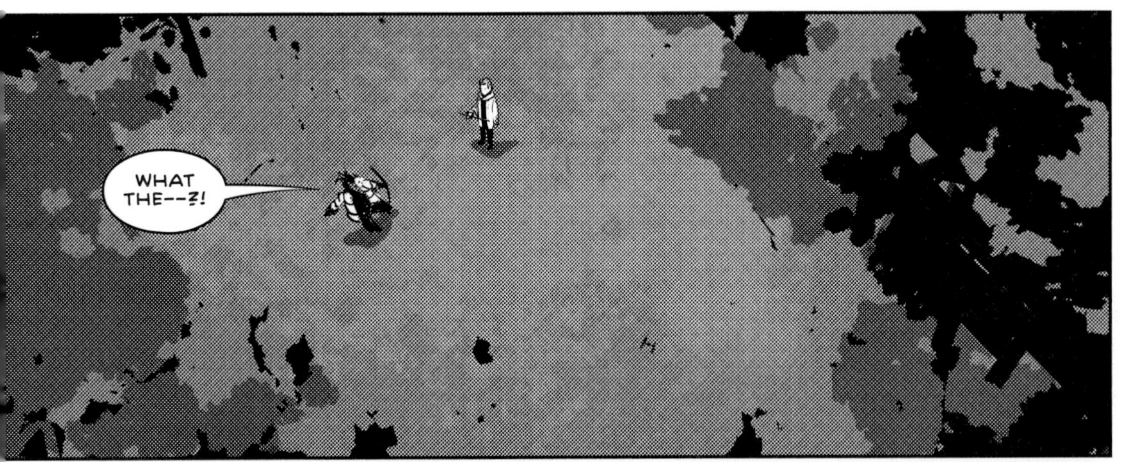
WHAT THE--?!

SHIT!

DADDY! DADDY, I--I KNOW I WASN'T SUPPOSED TO BUT I *FOLLOWED YOU*--

I'M SORRY! BUT I'M HERE AND I NEED HELP! WHERE ARE YOU?!

DADDY?
--DADDY?
KZZT
DADDY!
NO.
DADDY,
NO...

WHAT--
WHAT DID YOU DO TO HIM? *WHAT DID YOU DO TO MY DADDY?*

DON'T BE SCARED

THIS WAY... HE'S JUST OVER HERE.
--BETTER NOT BE LYING, BILLY.

WHAT-- WHO IS THAT?!

I'M NOT GOING WITH YOU! I'M ***NOT LEAVING MY DAD!***

WHAT? I--

--QUIT COMPLAINING, BATS. YOU'RE SO LAZY.
SHUT UP.
YOU SHUT UP!

BOTH OF YOU, BE QUIET...

SEE, I TOLD YOU.

THERE HE IS.

HOW COME... HOW COME YOU DON'T SEEM WORRIED?
IT'S LIKE WE SAID, ROMIE HAS LIVED LONGER THAN ANY OF US. THEY'LL BE OKAY.

NO, NOT JUST NOW. I MEAN, LIKE, YOU NEVER SEEM WORRIED. EVER.

THE WORLD ALREADY ENDED, YUI. WHAT ELSE CAN BE WORSE THAN THAT? WAY I SEE IT, EVERY DAY AFTER THAT HAS JUST BEEN A BONUS.

YEAH, BUT WHAT IF WHAT BILLY SAID *IS* TRUE?!
IT COULD CHANGE EVERYTHING! I MEAN I-- I LIKE THE WAY THINGS ARE. THEY'VE BEEN LIKE THIS FOR AS LONG AS WE CAN REMEMBER. I DON'T WANT IT TO CHANGE!

EVERYTHING CHANGES, YUI. EVENTUALLY. BUT WE'LL BE OKAY.
YOU THINK SO?
SURE I DO.

I AM KIND OF HUNGRY. DID YOU BRING ANY SNACKS?

THINK SO...

HERE.
THANKS.

I--I WANT SOME.
THEN HAVE SOME. IT'S *OKAY,* VICKIE. I PROMISE.
I DON'T KNOW-- I--
I'LL DO IT FIRST. I DON'T CARE.
NO! DON'T!
STOP IT! STOP BEING A BABY!
RAYMOND, DON'T!

NO...
NO...

HERE...
TRY...

DADDY...

THIS CAN'T BE REAL--IT CAN'T--

WHAT IS THIS?

WHAT *ARE* YOU?

THEY ARE THE CHILDREN.

THIS IS THE NIGHT.

1933.
YOU FIRST.
NO WAY! THIS WAS YOUR IDEA.
WAS NOT!
ebraska.
IT WAS, TOO! AND NOW YOU'RE CHICKENING OUT! YOU ALWAYS DO THIS!
I'M NOT CHICKENING OUT.
OKAY, WE GO TOGETHER THEN. COUNT OF THREE. DEAL?
...
FINE.
ONE... TWO...

THREE!
--UNGH!

I BROKE MY FISHING POLE!
IT WAS JUST A STICK. FIND ANOTHER ONE.

HOW ARE WE SUPPOSED TO CATCH ANY FISH NOW!
YOU WERE NEVER GOING TO **CATCH ONE** ANYWAYS! YOU KNOW **HOW MANY HOURS** I'VE SAT THERE WATCHING YOU WITH THAT DAMN FISHING POLE? ONLY TIME WE EAT IS WHEN I FIND US REAL WORK.
THINK THERE'LL BE ANY WORK HERE?
...
DON'T KNOW.

ANY BREAD LEFT?
NO. BEANS ARE GONE, TOO.

I'M HUNGRY, RAY.
I KNOW. ME, TOO. BUT WE KEEP MOVING EAST LIKE PA SAID. WE'LL BE OKAY.

I WISH WE'D STAYED HOME.
WE COULDN'T. MA AND PA COULDN'T BARELY FEED THOMAS AND SALLY AS IT WAS. WE'RE MEN NOW, RONNIE. WE JUST NEED TO FIND WORK. LOOK AFTER EACH OTHER.
JUST *SO HUNGRY* ALL THE TIME.
I KNOW HOW YOU FEEL. TO UNDERSTAND WHAT *REAL HUNGER* IS...
WHO'S THERE?!
WE AIN'T GOT NO FOOD. AIN'T GOT NO MONEY.

DON'T BE SCARED. I DON'T NEED FOOD.
DON'T NEED MONEY.
YOU DON'T NEED TO BE HUNGRY ANYMORE, EITHER.

RONNIE & RAYMOND.

OH... WOW.
I DON'T--I DON'T FEEL RIGHT.
JUST GIVE IT A MINUTE...

THERE... SEE?

YES!

I FEEL...
INCREDIBLE!

IT'S LIKE I CAN *REALLY SEE* AGAIN!

WHAT'S YOUR PROBLEM?!
NOTHING-- JUST FEELS *SO WEIRD.*

LIKE IT'S *TOO MUCH.* I--
LET'S GO HOME, RAY. LET'S GO TO SLEEP.

SLEEP?! ARE YOU CRAZY?! WE'VE *BEEN ASLEEP,* RONNIE.

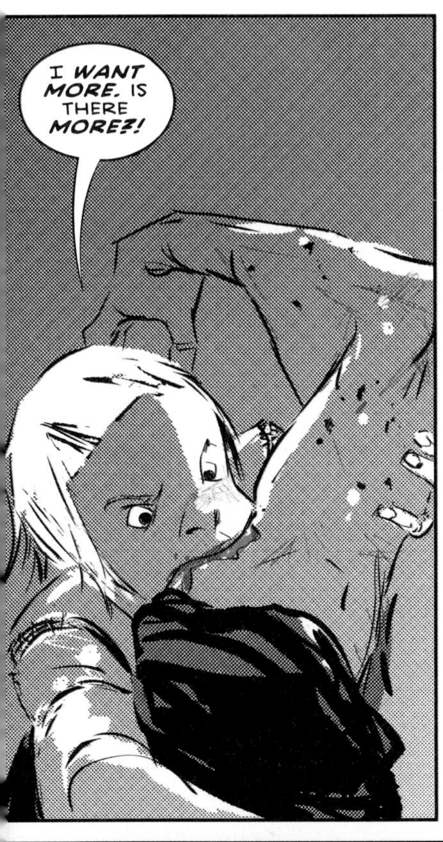
I WANT MORE. IS THERE MORE?!

THERE HAS TO BE MORE, RIGHT? I MEAN, THERE CAN'T JUST BE ONE LEFT.

RIGHT, BILLY?
QUIET. I'M THINKING.

THERE ARE MORE.
HOW DO YOU KNOW?

HE WAS TALKING TO SOMEONE.

HOW LONG HAVE YOU BEEN HERE?

HOW LONG HAVE YOU BEEN--LIKE THAT?

THIS CAN'T BE RIGHT--
THIS *ISN'T REAL!*

MY DAD. I WANT TO GO BACK TO MY DAD.

DON'T TOUCH ME!

GET *AWAY FROM ME!*

I'M GOING BACK TO MY DAD! AND I DON'T WANT YOU TO FOLLOW ME! UNDER-STAND?!

ROMIE WOULD NEVER HURT YOU...

ROMIE WOULD NEVER HURT ANYONE.

WOW. *SHE'S REAL.*
I'D FORGOTTEN... FORGOTTEN WHAT THEY SMELL LIKE.

STAY AWAY FROM ME!
IT'S OKAY...

DON'T FREAK OUT.
WE CAN HELP YOU.

I WANT MY DAD. I WANT TO *GO HOME.*

HOW FAR IS HOME?
I DON'T KNOW. I WASN'T EVEN SUPPOSED TO COME BUT I FOLLOWED MY DAD HERE ANYWAY.

MAYBE AN HOUR NORTH. SOMETHING LIKE THAT.
BUT I CAN'T-- I CAN'T LEAVE MY DAD. MAYBE HE'S OKAY. MAYBE HE JUST NEEDS FRANK TO LOOK AT HIM AND FIX HIM UP.

OKAY... LET'S GO SEE.

YOU SURE THEY'RE THIS WAY?
THIS IS THE WAY.
GUYS, THIS IS **TOO FAR.** WE SHOULD HEAD BACK SOON.

MAYBE HE'S RIGHT. THE SUN WILL BE UP IN A COUPLE OF HOURS.

SO, WE FIND SOMEWHERE ELSE TO SLEEP.

WAIT--WHAT DO YOU MEAN? WE CAN'T--OUR SLEEPING PLACES. WE NEED OUR SLEEPING PLACES.
YEAH, I MEAN--HE'S RIGHT. THEY SAID...

THEY SAID.
THEY SAID A LOT OF THINGS. THEY SAID THEY'D COME BACK FOR US.

THEY SAID THEY'D NEVER LEAVE US. HOW LONG AGO WAS THAT? SO LONG WE CAN'T EVEN REMEMBER.

YEAH, BUT OUR ***SLEEPING PLACES.*** WE CAN'T MOVE OUR SLEEPING PLACES, BILLY. THAT'S LIKE ***THE ONE RULE.***

WHAT IF THAT WAS ***A LIE?*** WHAT IF ***EVERYTHING*** THEY TOLD US WAS A LIE JUST TO ***KEEP US HERE?***

COME ON... IT'S NOT FAR NOW.

HEY, HOLD UP.
WHAT NOW?

DON'T YELL AT ME OR CALL ME A CHICKEN OR ANYTHING. BUT I'M SCARED, RAY...
YOU THINK IT'S TRUE? YOU THINK THEY LIED?

IT DOESN'T MATTER. IT'S JUST US NOW. IT'S GOING TO BE OKAY.
YOU SURE?
I PROMISE.

WAIT!
WHAT?

DO YOU SMELL THEM?

"THEY'RE CLOSE.
IS JOHN BACK?
NOPE. GIRL'S GONE, TOO.
I KNEW WE SHOULD NEVER HAVE LET LAURA GO AFTER HIM.
I'LL GO LOOK FOR 'EM AS SOON AS I FINISH HERE.

WHO--
WHO THE
HELL ARE
YOU?!

ARE--
YOU OKAY,
SWEETHEART?

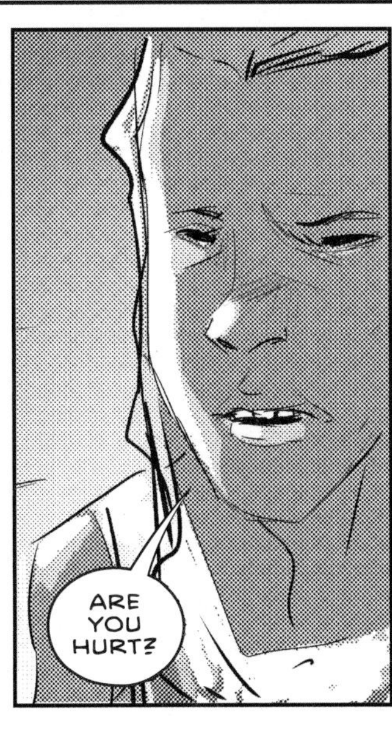
ARE
YOU
HURT?

CHANGE MAY START SLOWLY. BUT WHEN IT TAKES HOLD...
GAHHHRRRGH!
--FUCK!

THERE IS NO STOPPING IT.

IT CAN CONSUME. IT CAN **DEVOUR**...

AND YOU HAVE NO CHOICE BUT TO LET IT HAPPEN OR BE LEFT BEHIND.

THIS IS AMAZING!

COME ON, MAN! SEE?! SEE?!
YEAH-- YOU'RE RIGHT. I--IT FEELS AMAZING.

BUT NO CHANGE COMES WITHOUT A COST...
IT FEELS SO GOOD!

RONNIE?

1945.
Hiroshima.

<LOOK, CHILD...>
<...LOOK WHAT THEY DID.>

<EVEN I HAVE NEVER SEEN...>

<AH! AT LEAST I KNOW I CAN STILL CRY. THAT IS SOMETHING. YES?>
<AND YOU, CHILD. NOW YOU ARE ALONE.>
<NOW YOU HAVE SEEN. SEEN WHAT THEY ARE... WHAT THEY DO.>
<NO, NO... DON'T--DON'T BE SCARED.>
<YOU NEVER HAVE TO BE SCARED AGAIN.>

<COME THEN, LET'S LEAVE THIS PLACE OF DEATH. LET'S LEAVE ***ALL DEATH*** BEHIND.>
<YOU WILL NEVER BE ALONE AGAIN.>

YUI.

SHOULD WE HELP HER?

NO. I DON'T--I DON'T THINK WE SHOULD GET CLOSE AGAIN.

ME NEITHER. LIKE IT WAS PULLING ME... HIS BLOOD. EVEN THOUGH THERE WASN'T MUCH LEFT. I FELT--
AND I--I *LIKED IT,* LUCAS. THAT'S THE WORST PART. I *LIKED* HOW IT FELT.

ME TOO.
THAT'S WHY WE STAY UP HERE. WE *STAY AWAY.*

I JUST WANT IT TO GO BACK. I WANT TO BE IN MY LIBRARY. AND I WANT YOU TO WRITE YOUR SONGS AND FOR BATS AND VICKIE AND BILLY TO BE PLAYING CAPTURE THE FLAG AND RAYMOND AND RONNIE TO BE DOING THEIR STUPID STUNTS.

I DON'T WANT THIS. I *DON'T WANT* IT TO CHANGE.

EVERYTHING CHANGES EVENTUALLY, YUI. EVEN *US.*

DID YOU HAVE PARENTS? OR WERE YOU ALWAYS... *LIKE THIS?*

THEY DIED. WAS THAT DURING THE PANDEMIC? LIKE MOST OF THE OTHER PEOPLE?

LONG BEFORE THAT. A *LOT* LONGER.

I'M GOING TO CALL THE OTHERS.
DON'T WORRY, I WON'T--I WON'T TELL THEM ABOUT YOU. BUT I WANT THEM TO KNOW WHERE I AM. I'M GOING TO GO BACK NOW.

ARE YOU SURE THAT'S A GOOD IDEA? IT'S GOING TO BE LIGHT SOON.

SHE'S NOT SCARED OF THE LIGHT LIKE US, YUI.

OH... RIGHT.

HELLO? MARJORIE? FINNICK?

KSHHHHHHHHHH..
THAT'S WEIRD.

WHAT?! WHAT IS IT?

THE OTHERS... BILLY, VICKIE...

I THINK YOU BETTER COME WITH US, LAURA.

RONNIE...

FUCKING MONSTERS--

GARRGH!

--UNGH!

GET BACK! GET THE FUCK BACK!

HSSSS!

FUCK!
--GUH!

LET'S GO AFTER HIM!
NO!

WE--WE DON'T HAVE TIME. WE GOTTA GO BACK. WE HAVE AN HOUR, MAYBE TWO.

BUT I'M STILL HUNGRY, BILLY! I WANT HIM!
YEAH! WE SLEEP AROUND HERE. KEEP GOING, THERE WILL BE MORE. AND MORE...

I DON'T KNOW, BILLY... I WANT TO SLEEP IN MY OWN SPOT. I--I NEED TO.

YOU DON'T NEED TO. THAT'S IN YOUR HEAD. AND THERE IS NO FOOD BACK THERE!
WE CAN SLEEP ANYWHERE. WE CAN GO ANYWHERE!

MAYBE BATS IS RIGHT. I THINK WE SHOULD GO BACK. I--I WANT TO GO BACK, TOO.

FINE. BUT THEN WE FIGURE THIS OUT, WE HUNT. NO WAY I'M GOING BACK TO EATING *FUCKING RATS!*

GUYS, HELP ME... MAYBE HE WILL HEAL.

HE'S NOT HEALING, RAY. YOU *KNOW* HE'S NOT HEALING.

I'M *NOT* LEAVING HIM.

BILLY...
FINE. WE'RE GOING BACK. YOU BETTER FIND A PLACE TO SLEEP, RAY.

THIS--
THIS IS ALL YOURS?
YEAH, I GUESS. NO ONE ELSE REALLY EVER WANTS TO READ.

HOW LONG HAVE YOU GUYS BEEN HERE?

TOLD YOU, WE DON'T REMEMBER.
I KNOW, BUT I MEAN ***REALLY?*** YOU ***REALLY*** DON'T REMEMBER?

WHAT YEAR IS IT? DO YOU KNOW?

WELL, MY DAD AND FINNICK TRIED TO KEEP TRACK. DAD THOUGHT IT WAS TWENTY-THREE-TWENTY-FIVE BUT FINNICK SAID IT WAS TWENTY-THREE-TWENTY-EIGHT.

THREE HUNDRED...
THREE HUNDRED YEARS.

I--
WOW.

BUT-- AREN'T THERE MORE? AREN'T THERE GROWN-UPS LIKE YOU?

THERE WERE.
THEY BROUGHT US HERE. SAID PEOPLE DIDN'T COME HERE ANYMORE. SAID THEY'D COME BACK FOR US WHEN IT WAS SAFE.

WE'VE BEEN-- WE'VE BEEN *WAITING.*

WHAT IS IT, ROMIE?

THE OTHERS?
YEAH, THEY SHOULD BE BACK BY NOW.

WHAT IS GOING ON?!
IT'S TOO LATE TO GO LOOKING.

IT'S--THEY'LL BE OKAY. BILLY IS SMART. HE'LL MAKE SURE THEY GET BACK. BUT WE CAN'T STAY UP. NOT ANY LONGER.
HOW AM I SUPPOSED TO SLEEP KNOWING THEY'RE OUT THERE?!

EVERYTHING WILL WORK OUT. IT ALWAYS DOES.

YEAH... UNTIL IT DOESN'T ANYMORE.

THIS IS THE NIGHT AND THESE ARE THE CHILDREN.

BUT EVERY NIGHT HAS TO END.
AND EVERY CHILD HAS TO GROW UP.

EVEN THEM.

EVEN ME.

THAT FIRE HAD STARTED, BUT IT WOULD TAKE A WHILE TO BURN.
MOST KIDS ARE SCARED OF THE DARK. BUT NOT THESE.
THEY KNEW TO FEAR THE LIGHT...

YOU SEE, IT WAS IN BROAD DAYLIGHT THAT THE REAL DANGER WAS FREE TO MOVE.
SSSS...
--UNGH.

AS THE OTHERS SLEPT, THAT DANGER CREPT CLOSER.
I--I'M SORRY, RONNIE...

THAT WAS THE **NIGHT**, BUT THIS WAS **THE DAY**...
ARRRRGH!

...AND DAY WAS WHERE THE **REAL MONSTERS** LIVED.

--GUNGH!

I'M SORRY, RONNIE.

NOT YET YOU AIN'T...

BUT YOU WILL BE.

REST UP, KID, 'CAUSE SOON AS NIGHT COMES, YOU'RE GONNA TAKE ME BACK TO WHERE YOU ALL LIVE.
THEN I'M GONNA KILL ***EVERY LAST ONE OF YOU*** LITTLE BASTARDS.

HOW DOES FOREVER END?

DOES EVERYTHING JUST FADE OUT SLOWLY? SO SLOW YOU DON'T EVEN NOTICE UNTIL THERE'S ONLY DARK AND YOU'RE **GONE?**

OR DOES IT ALL END IN FEAR AND BLOOD AND SCREAMING?

MY MEMORIES OF THE END ARE ALL MIXED UP... I DON'T **TRUST THEM** ANYMORE.
I DON'T KNOW HOW FOREVER ENDS... BUT I KNOW IT WASN'T HERE. THEN...

...LET'S GO BACK A LITTLE FURTHER. SEE IF I CAN STILL REMEMBER CLEARLY... IN THE RIGHT ORDER...

LET'S GO BACK TO WHEN I WAS STILL ALL ALONE.

IT WOULD END AT NIGHT. IT WOULD END WITH A BITE.

BUT IT STARTED IN THE DAYLIGHT.

THAT WAS THE DAY I WALKED ALONE AND REALIZED, MAYBE FOR THE FIRST TIME, **HOW YOUNG** I REALLY WAS.

MY DAD AND FINN AND SOME OF THE OTHERS TALKED ABOUT THE OLD TIMES, EVEN THOUGH THEY HADN'T LIVED THROUGH THEM.

BUT THAT DAY I SAW IT... I SAW WHAT FOREVER **LOOKS LIKE...**

ALL THOSE YEARS.
ALL THOSE NIGHTS...
ALL PUT INTO
THOSE LINES.

OH!

BUT THIS STORY IS NOT MINE ALONE. EVEN IN BROAD DAYLIGHT, THINGS STILL STIRRED IN THE DARK...
HOW MANY MORE OF YOU ARE THERE?

HSSSSS!

ANSWER ME, KID, OR I SWEAR TO GOD I AM GONNA PUT THIS ARROW THROUGH YOUR EYE.

GO AHEAD. THINK THAT'LL STOP ME?

PROBABLY NOT...

BUT THIS MIGHT.
ARRRRGH!

C--CLOSE IT! *CLOSE IT!*
SURE. JUST GONNA MAKE SURE YOU'LL PLAY NICE FIRST.

YOU READY TO ANSWER SOME QUESTIONS, OR AM I GONNA HAVE TO OPEN THIS AGAIN?
YES... PLEASE...

NOW, TELL ME. ARE THE OTHERS STILL OUT THERE, WAITING TO GET ME WHEN I COME OUT, HUH?
NO. THEY LEFT. WENT BACK.

BACK *WHERE?*
THE CITY. THAT'S WHERE WE LIVE.

HOW MANY?

EIGHT OF US...

I MEAN, THERE *WERE* EIGHT OF US.

ALWAYS TOLD US TO STAY AWAY FROM THE CITY. NEVER KNEW WHY.

THEY TOLD US NEVER TO LEAVE.

THEY? THEY WHO?

THE OLD ONES. BUT THAT WAS A LONG TIME AGO.

REST UP. WE'RE MOVING AS SOON AS THE SUN GOES DOWN.
BILLY AND THE OTHERS WILL BE WAITING.

CHANGE OF PLANS... WE AIN'T GOING BACK TO THE CITY.
LEAST, NOT YET.

THAT DAY STRETCHED ON FOR A LONG TIME.
I KNOW IT WASN'T, BUT IT ALMOST FEELS LIKE THAT WAS THE **LAST DAY** NOW.
AT LEAST, THE LAST DAY I REMEMBER EVERYTHING BEING QUIET. BUT THERE WAS THIS FEELING TOO... A FEELING I'LL **NEVER FORGET.**
MAYBE I SHOULD HAVE BEEN MORE SCARED? IF I KNEW THEN WHAT I **KNOW NOW,** WOULD I HAVE STAYED? OR WOULD I RUN?

I WAS HOPING YOU'D BE UP SOON.

SO, THIS IS ALL YOURS? YOU DREW ALL THIS YOURSELF?

HOW--HOW LONG HAS THIS TAKEN?

RIGHT.

I STILL--I STILL CAN'T BELIEVE THIS IS REAL. THAT YOU'RE REAL.

CAN I ASK--WHAT HAPPENED? I MEAN, WHY DON'T YOU TALK?

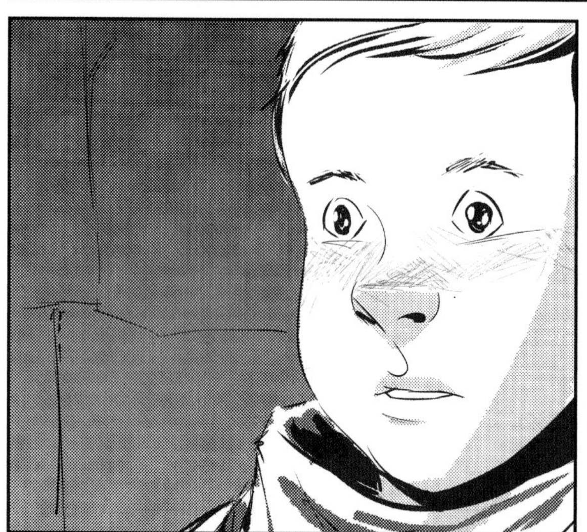

I DIDN'T MEAN TO-- I'M SORRY. WAIT UP!

ROMIE? YOU DON'T HAVE TO TELL ME ANYTHING YOU DON'T WANT TO, OKAY?

I JUST--I MISS MY DAD. AND I GUESS YOU'RE THE ONLY ONE I HAVE NOW AND--

MMRR?

I DON'T THINK THAT'S FAIR.
FAIR? SINCE WHEN IS ANYTHING FAIR, BATS?

ALL WE'RE SAYING IS THAT MAYBE WE DON'T TELL LUCAS AND YUI.
BUT WHY?

WELL, IF THERE ARE MORE OUT THERE...
SHE'S RIGHT. THERE CAN'T BE TOO MANY LEFT, RIGHT? MAYBE WE KEEP THEM FOR US?

BUT WE ALWAYS DO EVERYTHING TOGETHER.

WHAT OTHER CHOICE DID WE HAVE?

THINGS HAVE CHANGED. I MEAN *REALLY* CHANGED. WE CAN'T STOP NOW... NOT NOW THAT WE KNOW *WHAT IT'S LIKE.*

I'M--I'M ALREADY GETTING HUNGRY, GUYS. LIKE, *REALLY HUNGRY,* NOT LIKE BEFORE.

ME, TOO. I SAY WE GET OUR STUFF AND WE GO. WE START HUNTING AND WE DON'T STOP MOVING.

WE NEED TO FORGET HOW THINGS HAVE *ALWAYS BEEN* AND START THINKING ABOUT WHAT THEY *CAN BE.*

THERE YOU ARE! WE THOUGHT MAYBE YOU LEFT.
WHAT IS IT, ROMIE? WHAT'S WRONG?

THEY'RE COMING... THE OTHER KIDS.

WE NEED TO HIDE HER.

TAKE HER TO THE LIBRARY, ROMIE.

GO!

I STILL DON'T KNOW ABOUT MOVING OUR STUFF...
UGH! HOW MANY TIMES DO WE HAVE TO GO THROUGH THIS? THERE'S ONLY SO FAR WE CAN GO EACH NIGHT IF WE STAY HERE.
theater
TIN STARS

BUT--
BUT NOTHING. THIS IS THE WAY IT HAS TO BE.
WHAT HAS TO BE? WHERE WERE YOU GUYS?

I-- NOWHERE.

BATS...

WE FOUND FOOD. MORE FOOD.

BATS?! WHAT DID WE JUST TALK ABOUT?!
WHAT?! THEY'D FIND OUT ANYWAY!

FOOD... YOU MEAN *PEOPLE.*

YES, YUI. *PEOPLE.*

THEY TOLD US *NEVER* TO FEED ON PEOPLE! THEY MADE US *PROMISE!*

THEY TOLD US LOTS OF THINGS! AND *WHERE ARE THEY* NOW?

HEY, WAIT... WHERE ARE THE TWINS?

THERE-- THERE WAS AN ACCIDENT.

ACCIDENT? WHAT DO YOU MEAN **AN ACCIDENT?**

...

WHAT DID YOU DO?! **WHAT HAVE YOU GUYS DONE?!**

YOU HAVE **NO IDEA,** LUCAS... NO IDEA WHAT **IT'S LIKE**--WHAT THEY **KEPT** FROM US!

THEY KEPT US HERE.
THEY KEPT US **CHILDREN.**

THEY KEPT US **SAFE!**

SAFE FROM WHAT?
DON'T YOU GET IT, YUI? WE'RE THE DANGEROUS ONES.

WHERE ARE RONNIE AND RAYMOND?! WHAT HAPPENED?!

GET OFF OF ME. I SWEAR, LUCAS--GET OFF!

WAIT--
WHAT?

THAT-- THAT SMELL...

"...THEY HAVE ONE."

WHERE ARE THEY?! WHERE DID YOU HIDE THEM?!
YOU THINK WE'D TELL YOU?
ALL WE HAVE TO DO IS WAIT UNTIL SUNUP.

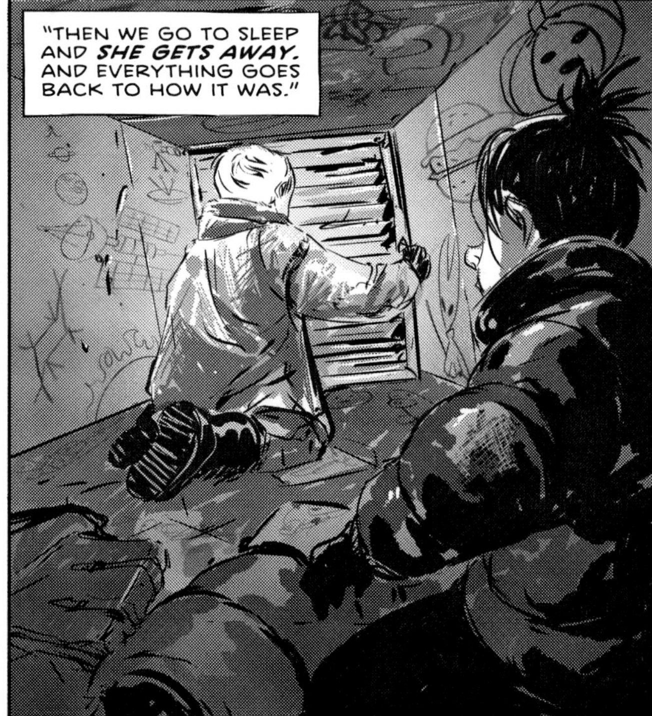
"THEN WE GO TO SLEEP AND SHE GETS AWAY. AND EVERYTHING GOES BACK TO HOW IT WAS."

NOW TELL US WHERE SHE IS OR ELSE.

OR ELSE, WHAT?

HSSSSSS!
OR ELSE WE KILL YOU TOO!